Disney · PIXAR

TOY STORY

PaRragon

Bath · New York · Cologne · Melbourne · Delhi
Hong Kong · Shenzhen · Singapore

Woody the cowboy was Andy's favourite toy. He lived in Andy's bedroom with Slinky Dog, Rex the dinosaur, Mr Potato Head, Hamm the pig, Bo Peep and all the other toys.

These toys were special. When no one was around, they came to life!

One day, Woody called all the toys together. "Andy and his family are moving to a new house soon," he told them. "That's why Andy's having his birthday party today."

The toys were worried. A birthday party meant new toys. What if Andy liked his new toys more than he liked them?

"One of us might be replaced!" groaned Rex.

"There's no need to worry," Woody promised. "Andy wouldn't do that."

As Andy unwrapped his presents, the toys waited nervously. Everything was fine until the very last present – a brand-new spaceman! Andy brought him up to the bedroom and left him there.

"I'm Buzz Lightyear, space ranger," the new toy said.

Woody couldn't help but feel jealous. "You're NOT a space ranger," he said. "You're just a toy like the rest of us!"

But all of the other toys thought
Buzz was wonderful and so did Andy.
Woody felt left out.

One day, Woody came up with a plan to stop Buzz getting
all of Andy's attention. He thought that if he aimed the remote
control car at Buzz, the new toy would fall behind the desk
and Andy wouldn't be able to find him. But the car sped out of
control and everything went wrong – Buzz fell out of the window!

"It was an accident!" said Woody. But none of the toys would
believe him.

Suddenly, Andy burst into the room. He was going to Pizza Planet and wanted to take a toy.

"I can't find Buzz, Mum," he called. "I'll have to take Woody instead."

But Buzz did go with them! He had fallen into a bush and grabbed hold of the car just as it drove away.

Pizza Planet was full of arcade games. Buzz, who still believed he was a real space ranger, thought one game was a spaceship. He crawled inside and Woody followed him.

The game was full of toy aliens that were picked up by a claw. Suddenly, the claw grabbed Buzz! Woody held onto Buzz's foot and he was horrified when he saw who had grabbed them – it was Sid, Andy's cruel neighbour.

Back in Sid's bedroom, Woody and Buzz were terrified. They were surrounded by weird-looking mutants that Sid had made from toys that he had broken. The mutant toys crawled closer and closer towards Woody and Buzz.

"Get back, you savages!" cried Woody. "Buzz, come on, we've got to get out of here – fast!"

They had just escaped when Buzz heard a voice calling:
"Come in, Buzz Lightyear, this is Star Command."
Buzz left Woody hiding in a cupboard and ran towards the voice.
But it was only a television advertisement for the Buzz Lightyear toy.
Buzz was stunned. "Is it true?" he whispered. "Am I really ... a toy?"

Desperate to prove he was a real space ranger, Buzz tried to fly out of a window in Sid's house. But instead he crashed to the floor and his arm broke off.

Woody found Buzz and took him back to
Sid's room. Looking out of Sid's window, he
saw his old friends in Andy's room.

"Hey guys, help!" Woody called to them,
waving madly.

But the toys thought Woody had hurt
Buzz again. Woody turned away sadly
from the window – it seemed that he and
Buzz were on their own.

Later on, Sid burst into the room. He grabbed Buzz and tied a big rocket to his back. "Tomorrow I'm sending you to infinity and beyond!" he sniggered.

That night, Buzz was sad. "You were right," he told Woody. "I'm not a space ranger. I'm just a toy."

"But being a toy is what makes you special," said Woody. "You're Andy's toy and he thinks you're great. He needs us and we have to get back to him!"

"You're right!" Buzz said at last.

But it was too late! BRRRRRRING rang Sid's alarm clock.

"Today's the day, spaceman," Sid said. He took Buzz downstairs and into the garden, where he started to build a launchpad. Woody turned to Sid's toys for help. They had to come up with a plan to rescue Buzz!

Out in the garden, Sid was ready to light the fuse on Buzz's rocket. "Ten! Nine! Eight ..." he counted.

Suddenly, Sid heard something. "Reach for the sky!" called a voice. It was Woody, lying nearby. Sid turned and stared. He picked up Woody. How did the cowboy doll get outside? Was there something wrong with its pull-string?

Then, one by one, the mutant toys stood up and staggered towards Sid! Together, they surrounded the stunned boy.

Woody wasn't done with Sid yet.

"From now on, you must take good care of your toys," he warned.
"Because if you don't, we'll find out, Sid." And then he leaned in very close:
"So play nice!"

"AAAHH!" Sid threw up his arms and shrieked in terror. He ran into
the house screaming. The toys cheered – their plan had worked! Buzz was
saved! And best of all, Sid's days of torturing toys were over.

But Woody and Buzz couldn't stand around and cheer – it was the day that Andy was moving house!

Quickly, the two toys ran towards home. But Buzz couldn't fit through the fence with the rocket still attached to his back. Woody wouldn't leave without his new friend. By the time Woody helped Buzz through the fence, though, it was too late. Andy's car had driven off.

Woody and Buzz ran after the moving van, determined to catch up. Buzz managed to grab a loose strap and climb up. He tried to help Woody up, too. "Come on! You can do it, Woody!" Buzz shouted.

But Scud, Sid's mean dog, had raced after them. Scud leaped up and grabbed Woody in his mouth.

"Nooooo!" Buzz yelled. He jumped onto Scud's head to save Woody.

Now Woody was safe, but Buzz was left behind, caught in Scud's jaws. Woody found RC Car in the back of the van and, using the remote control, sent RC back to pick up Buzz. But the other toys didn't understand what Woody was doing and angrily threw him off the van!

Luckily, Buzz and RC picked up Woody as they came speeding back. Finally realizing what was going on, the other toys tried to help ...

... but RC's batteries ran out!

Then they realized Buzz still had the rocket on his back!
Once lit, the rocket zoomed all three of them forwards.
RC landed in the van, while Woody and Buzz whooshed
into the sky. Just as the rocket was about to explode,
Buzz snapped open his space wings and broke free.

"Buzz, you're flying!" Woody cried.

"This isn't flying," Buzz replied.
"This is falling with style!"

While Andy was looking out the window, the two friends dropped unnoticed through the car's open sunroof, landing safely on the back seat.

Hearing a thump, Andy looked over. "Woody! Buzz!" he shouted. He hugged them close, thrilled to have his two favourite toys back.

Woody and Buzz had made it home.

Everyone settled happily into the new house. But all too soon, it was Christmas – which meant new toys.

They listened as Andy unwrapped his first present ... and suddenly their eyes widened as they heard an unmistakable sound: woof-woof!